ce

Aunt Nasty

There are lots of Early Reader
stories you might enjoy.

Look at the back of the book or,
for a complete list, visit
www.orionchildrensbooks.com

Aunt Nasty

Margaret Mahy

Illustrated by
Chris Mould

Orion
Children's Books

Aunt Nasty originally appeared in
The Third Margaret Mahy Storybook
first published by J M Dent & Sons Ltd in 1973
This Early Reader edition first published in Great Britain in 2015
by Orion Children's Books
a division of Hachette Children's Books
and published by Hodder and Stoughton Limited

Carmelite House
50 Victoria Embankment
London EC4Y 0DZ
An Hachette UK Company

1 3 5 7 9 10 8 6 4 2

Text © Margaret Mahy 1973
Illustrations © Chris Mould 2015

The paper and board used in this paperback are natural and
recyclable products made from wood grown in sustainable forests.
The manufacturing processes conform to the environmental
regulations of the country of origin.

A catalogue record for this book is available from the British Library.

ISBN 978 1 4440 1442 6

Printed and bound in China

www.orionchildrensbooks.com

Dedicated to all the marvellous
aunts and witches out there – C.M.

Contents

Chapter One

"Oh dear!" said Mum, one lunch time, after she had read a letter the postman had just left.

"What's the matter?" asked Dad.

Even Toby and Claire looked up from their boiled eggs.

"Aunt Nasty has written to say she is coming to stay with us," said Mum. "The thought of it makes me worried."

"You must tell her we will be out!" cried Toby. He did not like the sound of Aunt Nasty.

"Or say we have no room," said Dad.

"You know I can't do that," said Mum.

"Remember Aunt Nasty is a witch."

Toby and Claire looked at each other with round eyes.

They had forgotten that Aunt Nasty was a witch as well as an aunt. If they said there was no room Aunt Nasty might be very cross.

She might turn them into frogs.

"She's coming on the plane tomorrow," said Mum, looking at the letter. "It is hard to read. She writes with a magpie's feather and all the letters look like broomsticks."

"I see she has written it on mouse skin," said Dad.

"Isn't she just showing off?"
asked Toby. "If she was a real
witch she would ride a broomstick
here . . .

. . . not come by plane."

Claire had to move into Toby's
room so that Aunt Nasty would
have a bedroom all to herself.

She put a vase of flowers in
the room, but they were not
garden flowers. Aunt Nasty liked
poisonous flowers.

"Leave the cobwebs in that corner," said Dad.

"Remember how cross she was when you swept them down last time. She loves dust and cobwebs. All witches do."

Chapter Two

The next afternoon they went to the airport to meet Aunt Nasty.

It was easy to see her in the crowd getting off the plane.

She was an old sort of witch, all in black with a pointed hat and a broomstick.

"Hello, Aunt Nasty," said Mum.
"How nice to see you again."

"I don't suppose you are really pleased to see me," said Aunt Nasty. "But that doesn't matter.

There is a special meeting of
witches in the city this week.
That is why I had to come.

I will be out every night on my broom, and trying to sleep during the day. I hope the children are quiet."

"Why didn't you come on your broom, Aunt Nasty?" asked Toby. "Why did you have to come by plane?"

"Don't you ever listen to the weather report on the radio?" said Aunt Nasty crossly. "It said there would be gale force winds at midday.

Even the silly plane bucked around. I began to think they'd put us into a wheelbarrow by mistake. Two people were sick."

"Poor people," said Claire.

"Serve them right!" Aunt Nasty muttered.

When they got home Aunt Nasty went straight to her room. She smiled at the flowers, but she did not say thank you.

"I will have a catnap," she said, stroking the raggy black fur collar she wore.

"I hope the bed is not damp or lumpy. I used to enjoy a damp bed when I was a young witch, but I'm getting old now."

Then she shut the door.

They heard her put her suitcase against it.

"What a rude aunt!" said Toby.

"She has to be rude, because of being a witch," said Mum.

"Now, be nice quiet children, won't you! Don't make her cross or she might turn you into tadpoles."

The children went out to play, but they were not happy.

"I don't like Aunt Nasty," said Claire.

"I don't like having a witch in the house," said Toby.

Chapter Three

The house was very, very quiet and strange while Aunt Nasty was there. Everyone spoke in whispers and went around on tiptoe most of the time.

Once she came out of her room and asked for some toadstools. Toby found some for her under a pine tree at the top of the hill …

Aunt Nasty was not pleased with them.

"These are dreadful toadstools," she said. "They look good but they are disappointing. The brown, slimy ones are much better. But I suppose I will have to make do with them."

That was on Tuesday. Some
smoke came out of the keyhole
on Wednesday.

On Thursday Aunt Nasty broke
a soup plate.

However, they did not see her again until Friday. Then she came out and complained that there was not enough pepper in the soup.

At last it was Sunday.

Aunt Nasty had been there a week. Now she was going home again – this time by broomstick.

Toby and Claire were very
pleased.

Mum was pleased too, but she
looked tired and sad.

She went out to take some
plants to the woman next door.

While she was out Dad came in to the front garden suddenly.

"Do you know what?" he said to Toby and Claire. "I have just remembered something. It is your mum's birthday today and we have forgotten all about it.

We must go and buy birthday
presents at once."

"A present!" said a voice.
"Who wants a present?"

It was Aunt Nasty with her
suitcase, a broomstick and a big
black cat at her heels.

"Oh, look at the cat!" cried
Claire.

"I did not know you had a cat, Aunt Nasty."

"He sits around my neck when we travel," said Aunt Nasty proudly. "It is his own idea, and it is a good one, because people think he's a fur collar and I do not have to buy a ticket for him."

"But what is this I hear? Have you really forgotten to get your mum a birthday present?"

"I'm afraid we have!" said Dad sadly.

"Ha!" said Aunt Nasty fiercely.

"Now I never ever forgot my mum's birthday. Once I gave her the biggest rat you ever saw."

"I don't think Mummy would like a rat," said Claire.

"I wasn't going to give her one!" snapped Aunt Nasty.

"Tell me, can you draw?"

"Yes," said Toby and Claire.

"Can you draw a birthday cake, jellies, little cakes, sandwiches, roast chickens, bottles of fizzy lemonade, balloons, crackers, pretty flowers, birds and butterflies . . . and presents too?"

"Yes," said Toby and Claire.

"Well then, you draw them,"
said Aunt Nasty. "And I will cook
up some magic.

Where is the oven? Hmmm!
It is a bit on the clean side, isn't it?
An old black stove is much better
for a witch.

But, I will work something out,
you see if I don't."

Chapter Four

Claire drew and Toby drew. They covered lots and lots of pages with drawings of cakes and balloons and presents.

Aunt Nasty came in with a smoking saucepan. "Give me your drawings," she said. "Hurry up, I haven't got all day. Hmmmm! They aren't very good, are they? But they'll have to do. A good witch can manage with a scribble if she has to."

She popped the drawings into the saucepan.

A thick blue smoke filled the room.

No one could see anyone else.

"This smoke tastes like birthday cake," said Claire.

"It tastes like jelly and ice-cream," said Toby.

The smoke began to go up the chimney.

"I smell flowers," said Dad.

Then they saw that the whole room was changed.

Everywhere there were leaves and flowers and birds only as big as your little fingernail.

The table was covered with jellies of all colours, and little cakes and sandwiches. There was a trifle and two roast chickens.

All around the table were
presents and crackers and balloons
– so many of them they would
have come up to your knees.

"Aha!" said Aunt Nasty, looking
pleased. "I haven't lost my touch
with a bit of pretty magic."

Best of all was the birthday cake.

It was so big there was no room for it on the table.

The balloons bounced and
floated around the room.

The tiny birds flew everywhere
singing.

"What is in this parcel?" asked
Claire, pointing to a parcel that
moved and rustled. "Is it a rat?"

"It's two pigeons," said Aunt
Nasty.

"There is a pigeon house for
them in one of the other parcels.

Well, I must be off. I've wasted enough time."

"Won't you stay and wish Mummy a happy birthday?" asked Toby. "She would like to say thank you for her birthday party."

"Certainly not!" said Aunt Nasty.
"I never ever say thank you
myself. I don't expect anyone to
say it to me. I love rudeness, but
that is because I am a witch. You
are not witches, so make sure you
are polite to everyone."

She tied her suitcase to her broomstick and her cat climbed onto her shoulder.

"Goodbye to you anyway," she said.

"I don't like children, but you are better than most. Perhaps I will see you again or perhaps I won't."

She got on her broomstick
and flew out of the window, her
suitcase bobbing behind her. She
was a bit wobbly.

Chapter Five

"Well," said Dad, "she wasn't so bad after all. It will be strange not to have a witch in the house anymore."

"Mum will love her birthday,"
said Claire. "It was good of Aunt
Nasty. It is the prettiest party I
have ever seen."

"I don't even mind if she visits
us again next year," said Toby.

"Look, there is Mum coming now," said Dad.

"Let's go and meet her."

They all ran into the sunshine shouting "Happy Birthday!"

Toby had a quick look up in the air for Aunt Nasty.

There, far above him, he saw a tiny little black speck that might have been a seagull. He wasn't quite sure.

Then he took one of Mum's hands, and Claire took the other, and they pulled her, laughing and happy, up the steps into her birthday room.

What are you going to read next?

Have more adventures with
Horrid Henry,

or save the day with Anthony Ant!

Become a
superhero with *Monstar,*

float off to
sea with
Algy,

or have your very own Pirates' Picnic.

Grow carrots with

Lottie and Dottie,

make magic with The Witch Dog,

and cast a spell with The Three Little Magicians.

Enjoy all the Early Readers.